Dash Decides Going Potty is Awesome

A BOOK FOR KIDS WITH POTTY ANXIETY

Dash Learns Life Skills Series

To my Mom, Sharol
Thank you for all of the hours you spent reading
to me when I was growing up!

Dash was so excited to be at
Obedience School with his friends.

Dash's teacher, Mr. Zach, taught the puppies
all about toys and how to play.

Dash was having a hard time concentrating.
He had to go potty.

He didn't want to go at school and thought
he could wait until he got home.

Dash and his friends lined up
for the bus.

Dash hoped he could hold it
until he got home.

Mama said, "Welcome home, Dash!
Did you have fun at school?"

But Dash ran past Mama without answering her.

He couldn't stop to talk.
He had to go potty, NOW!

Dash ran through the house to the potty.

Dash was so relieved to have made it!

Mama asked, "Dash what happened?"

Dash said, "I didn't want to go potty at school.
But, I almost didn't make it!"

Mama said, "Dash, it isn't good to hold it until you get home!"

The next day, Mama needed to run errands and get groceries.

Dash asked, "Mama, can we get a treat
after we get groceries?"

Mama said, "That would be fun. Let's see how we feel after we're done with our shopping."

Dash hoped they felt up to it!

"Dash, why are you spinning in circles?" asked Mama.
"Do you have to go potty?"

"No Mama," said Dash. "I'm just having fun."

"Are you sure?" asked Mama.

"Yes, Mama!" said Dash.

Dash felt a little funny but as long as he was running and spinning he was ok.

Dash and Mama finished shopping and were at the register when Dash realized he had to go potty.

"Oh no!" said Dash.

"Mama! I have to go potty right NOW!"

The cashier told Mama that she would watch her cart while Mama took Dash to the bathroom.

Dash ran to the potty.

The potty had an automatic flush.
Dash was nervous that it would be loud
or flush when he wasn't ready.

Everything went great!

Dash wasn't scared
by the flush at all!

Dash didn't like loud paw dryers.

Mama assured him that she was right there and that he'd be okay.

Dash did a great job drying his paws.

Mama was very proud of him!

Mama and Dash checked out their groceries.

They stopped to get an ice cream on the way home to celebrate how well Dash had done going potty.

Dash decided that
Going Potty is Awesome!

If you enjoyed
Dash Decides Going
Potty is Awesome!
you might like these
books about Dash, too!

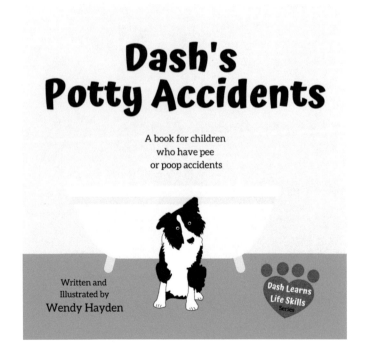

Made in United States
Troutdale, OR
01/26/2024

17138703R00021